Every Day is Christmas

May these stories
warm your heart

♡

Sandra Fischer

OTHER BOOKS BY SANDRA FISCHER

Seasons in the Garden

My Faithbook Messages—Devotions to Like and Share

Every Day is Christmas

STORIES TO WARM HEART AND SOUL BY

Sandra Fischer

ILLUSTRATED BY

Becky Guinn

Contents

Introduction

ver since the first Christmas, people have been sharing stories about what happened in a dusty stable in Bethlehem. That most marvelous event—the birth of Jesus, the Savior of the World—has stirred the hearts of poets, artists, and musicians. All have struggled to express the magnitude of God's love demonstrated by His coming to earth in human form to save us, reconcile us, and redeem us.

As a writer, I have also been drawn to share stories about Christmas, many of them true stories from my own past. The earliest Christmas memory I can recall was celebrating with a small Christmas tree set on a platform in front of our living room window. Around it lay an oval Lionel train track and village scene my father had built. What fun we had watching the little engine puffing "smoke" and whistling as it pulled the cars around the tree!

On Christmas day we would exchange gifts and enjoy a delicious meal of turkey and all the accompaniments. Growing up, my family's celebrations were mainly cultural, and it wasn't until I began attending church at age twelve that I learned that there was more to Christmas than those sweet, simple traditions. Oh, I had heard that Christmas was about Jesus' birth, but I did not know Him personally or understand why He had been born.

Meeting the Christ of Christmas changed my life. While I still enjoy and practice traditions embedded in the cultures of all the places I have lived, more than anything I want to honor the Christ of Christmas in the stories I write, the relationships I have, and the intimate spiritual journey of my soul. I want His story to be prime and to shine through all the trappings so that others will also

EVERY DAY IS CHRISTMAS

want to meet Him and accept the indescribable gift God gave us when He gave us Jesus.

Christmas story books abound, so I wondered how mine might have significance in the ocean of ink spilled in stories already published. I prayed about getting an illustrator to bring my words to life. I knew the internet was replete with talented people who could illustrate the stories competently, but I wanted someone who knew Jesus and would render the art to warm hearts and souls.

Becky Guinn came to mind. She was a talented Christian artist I knew through her sister-in-law, Katherine Bilbee. Katherine served as manager of Glad Tidings Books 'N Gifts, the store I owned before I retired. Through her, I knew Becky's life story and had heard what an amazing artist she was. I contacted Becky about illustrating my book; the email had barely rested in my outbox when Becky replied that she had been praying about what God would have her do next. He answered her prayer and mine!

The beauty of Becky's art speaks for itself, but what makes her illustrations even more remarkable is that her hands were amputated a few years ago. She creates all of her art with prosthetic "hands." Her life and work are a testament to God's mercy and miraculous power, just like Christmas itself. Please read more of her story at the end of this book.

As you go through this collection of stories—some real, some imagined— may they help you reconnect with the memories you hold in your heart's treasury. May you experience the deep range of emotions Christmas brings—love, happiness, sadness, regret, hope. Most of all, may you perceive the joy the Christ of Christmas brings to us each and every day and know that "Every Day is Christmas."

ii

Every Day is Christmas

A Christmas Pudding for Willie

Mary folded and refolded the bread dough, working it with rhythmic motions. Making bread was exhilarating for her. The possibilities in the unbaked loaf were like rising hopes, hopes for Christmas joy to come back to Ashworth Hall. She hummed a carol as she finished kneading and wiped her hands on her apron.

"McGarvey!" she shouted out the back door. "Come now and take a turn stirring the pudding."

A ruddy visage with reddened cheeks entered the warm kitchen refuge, rubbing his hands to thaw them. He shook his head, pressed his lips together and closed his eyes.

"Won't do a lick a good, Mum. She ain't about to 'ave Christmas dinner, let alone the pudding."

Mary lifted the cover and drank in the mixed aroma of the twenty-some ingredients in the bowl. She loved making the Christmas pudding; she called it "advent" food, a way of bringing together all the good things of life to be savored and enjoyed. It was like sharing the same love God did that first Christmas when Jesus was born. That was part of the reason the pudding had been Willie Ashworth's favorite aspect of Christmas too.

The dessert took days to ripen, growing richer with each person who was invited to stir it and make a wish. Mary enlisted everyone—the dustman, the postman, the carriage driver—all willing to oblige, particularly when she thanked them with fresh-baked scones. She added a  little stout for moisture and handed McGarvey the spoon.

"Stir," she commanded. "And make a wish. Better yet, be prayin' for Lady Ashworth."

McGarvey stirred, but he wasn't sure how to pray. "How do you pray for someone whose only child died of that awful cholera? How does God restore the loss of the life and laughter the boy brought to his mum, dad, and all us servants?"

Mary wiped her floury hands on her apron. "We must trust the Lord. He knows how to help. Just pray as best you can."

Cholera had swept through the country, taking its toll and paying no homage to age or status. If any mercy could be claimed for eight-year-old Willie Ashworth, it was his dying quickly and bravely.

"Mumsy, don't fear," he had told his mother on his final day. "I won't be alone. There'll be other boys in heaven, just like here, and angels to care for me.

4

I'll be with Jesus for Christmas, and maybe they'll have Christmas pudding too. Promise you'll think of me enjoying Christmas pudding in heaven."

The epidemic had passed, taking Willie and thousands with it and leaving desolate survivors like the Ashworths. Lord Ashworth buried his sadness in work, spending more time away to escape the emptiness; Lady Ashworth remained in her room, a willing prisoner, shackled by inconsolable grief.

"God help the missus... master too. Stir the joy back into their hearts." McGarvey's prayer was broken by a loud cackling from the henhouse outside.

"Not again!" He bolted out the door, rushed to the coop, and grabbed the egg-stealing ruffian by the collar before he could slip away. "Caught ya red-handed this time!"

The boy wriggled and squealed. "Please, mister, I only took two, just enough for supper for me brother and me. Have a heart. It's Christmas!"

McGarvey knew the boy was one of many street urchins orphaned by the epidemic; he knew too, that if word got out of any generosity, there'd be no end to it. He tightened his grip on the boy's coat.

Tears streamed down the boy's face as he screamed, "Help me, God!"

"Stop!"

The boy's body grew limp in McGarvey's hands as they both followed the sound of the voice. McGarvey recognized the pale countenance leaning out a second story window. "Bring him inside," she commanded. As always, he obeyed.

The pan of bread dough fell from Mary's hand as she stood in disbelief. Through one door came McGarvey with the urchin and through the other came Lady Ashworth.

"Are you an angel, come to save me?" the boy blurted.

"Perhaps." Lady Ashworth's voice was as soft as the young boy's cheek to the touch of her hand. *Perhaps he was an angel come to save her.* "How old are you?"

"Nine, ma'am, and I'm strong. I can work to pay for the eggs. My brother and me's all alone…" He sniffed and rubbed his eyes.

With a kerchief that held thousands of her own, she dried his tears. "Do you like Christmas pudding?"

"Ain't sure. Never had it. Is it as good as porridge?"

"Ten times better. Mary, set two more places for Christmas dinner."

"Make that three." Lord Ashworth stood in the doorway.

After dinner on Christmas day, Mary served the pudding to the Ashworths and the two young orphan boys. The evening—and the pudding—was full of love and redemption and hope, all stirred in and flavored with joy.

"Enjoy, Willie," Lady Ashworth whispered, as the two orphan boys filled the room with laughter. Although, if you had asked her, she could have sworn she heard the familiar tinkling glee of a third.

Seeing Christmas Through the Eyes of Children

I don't want to die. I just want to see Christmas."

I put down the newspaper and cried. A first grader spoke those words as she huddled in a bathroom with her classmates and teacher while a gunman stalked Sandy Hook elementary school. She was spared and would live to see Christmas; twenty other students and eight adults from the school would not.

As I searched for words to pray, the lyrics of a Christmas song I had heard recently came to mind. It was inspired by a child asking his mother why there was a line to see Santa at the mall, but no line to see Jesus.[1] I was struck by how those words—"Where's the line to see Jesus?"—cut to the core of what Christmas should be. *Oh, how we need to see Christmas—the Christ of Christmas, Jesus.* I wept again.

I thought back to that first Christmas when the shepherds had one quest in mind—to find the manger where the Christ child lay so they could worship him.

---

[1] The song, "Where's the Line to See Jesus," was written by Steve Haupt and Chris Loesch and is performed by Steve Haupt's daughter, Becky Kelley. It was inspired by their grandson, Spencer Reijers.

I, on the other hand, along with millions who profess to know and worship Christ, had just spent a whole day shopping for gifts to give to people. It wasn't even their birthday; it was Jesus'. The only line I looked for was the shortest at the checkout.

I was ashamed. The Sandy Hook schoolchild and the boy at the mall were two little children, unencumbered by culture and blessed with transparent honesty. They were unafraid to speak their hearts. On the other hand, I had become caught up in the web of cultural correctness and all the trappings of "holiday hysteria." I succumbed to making Christmas all about modern trimmings. I decorated a tree with little thought of the One who died on a barren tree for me. I carefully wrapped presents in bright colors for my children while the mother of my Savior had humbly swaddled the Son in common cloths. I graced our mantel with figures of the nativity, yet I shrank from speaking to unsaved guests about the centerpiece of the display, the Gift of God that could give them eternal life.

Was there ever a time such as this when I—when we—needed to see, really *see* Jesus? Children are seeking him—looking for Him amidst terror-filled moments, among frenzied shoppers and Santa-seekers. And He is always ready to reveal Himself to all who seek Him. I picture those Sandy Hook children who were killed, *seeing* Him face-to-face in heaven, while their grieving families seek comfort for their loss. I see the little boy who asked where the Jesus' line was, *seeing* Him and discovering Emmanuel, God with us, ever present in the hearts of all who believe.

How wonderful to open our hearts to see Jesus, to worship Him, to share the reason for His coming, and to be filled with a moment-by-moment awareness of His presence.

LORD, please give me the eyes and heart of a child today—to see You, to celebrate You, and proclaim You, the Christ of Christmas, to this world.

The Gift

J acob stood staring at the Christmas display in Gilley's General Store window. One item overshadowed all the others; to him, the Schwinn Autocycle with its shiny red and gold fenders eclipsed the dolls, toy trains, tools, and latest household items. A tag hung on the handlebars. Jacob read it every day when he walked by on his morning paper route: "Limited quantity, order now."

Mr. Gilley stepped out the door to get his paper. "Looking her over again, are we?"

"Yes sir. It's a nice bike." Jacob shifted his paper bag from one shoulder to the other.

"Still time to order. I'm saving that one to sell on Christmas eve. Of course, we have gifts for everyone. Your mother has admired that Singer sewing machine many times."

"Yes sir, you have mighty fine gifts, Mr. Gilley. See you tomorrow." Jacob took a notebook from his pocket and looked at the figures scribbled in it. If he was calculating correctly, he would have enough saved from his route and his holiday bonuses to get the bicycle on Christmas eve.

He closed his eyes for a moment. Instantly he was gliding along, with only the pleasant sound of the spokes whirring. He began to run, imagining the wind against his face, his knees rising high in a sprint as if he were pedaling the Autocycle. His paper bag flopped against his hip and he stopped to catch his breath. He reminded himself that with the bicycle he could deliver more papers and make enough to help Mama with the bills too.

When he arrived home his mother was sitting at her treadle machine, her feet working the pedal and her fingers pushing cloth under the needle. She stopped long enough to tell Jacob there were warm biscuits in the oven for him.

"You look a little flushed, son. Are you feeling alright?"

"I'm fine, Mama. Besides, it's too close to Christmas to get sick, and I need to do my route every day."

"You're a good boy, Jacob. I'm blessed to have you."

"I know, Mama." Jacob looked up at the photo above the sewing machine, a daily reminder. "I miss him too." The solemn eyes of his father in uniform stared at him from behind the framed glass. A handwritten inscription below the photo read: "Beloved husband and father, PFC. Allen Winters, U.S. Army, killed in action for his country, April 15, 1944. May he rest in peace."

Three long years had passed since Allen Winters died, leaving Jacob and his mother to manage as best they could. Without a formal education, Molly Winters applied her sewing skills to make apparel for families willing to hire her. Jacob helped by delivering the morning paper to as many patrons as he could enlist. His mother allowed him to keep a small portion of his earnings to spend on things of his choice. He usually saved it for Christmas.

Molly looked up from her sewing machine to see Jacob looking at his account book. She smiled. "Are you figuring again?"

"Yes ma'am. By Christmas I'll have enough for the bicycle and I'll be able to add more patrons. Maybe we'll have meat every day for our potato stew."

Molly stood up and stretched her arms. She reached over and poked Jacob in the ribs. "Doesn't look like you're any skinnier for walking, son."

Jacob laughed. "I will be when I whiz through town on my Autocycle."

The next day Jacob went with his mother to Gilley's to buy yard goods. Jacob tugged her arm and stopped at the window display.

"Isn't it a beauty?"

"Yes, it is," Molly said, but as Jacob turned to look at her face, he saw her eyes weren't on the bike. She was gazing at the Singer electric sewing machine displayed next to it. She grabbed his hand and turned away. "Come, let's do our shopping."

Christmas Eve came and Mr. Gilley gave Jacob the good news: he would be bringing Jacob's gift by in the morning after church because he had too many to deliver that evening. Jacob pumped the man's hand and smiled. "This is going to be the best Christmas ever!"

"I think so too, Jacob."

The next day Jacob sprinted to the door to meet Mr. Gilley, who stood holding the handlebars of the Autocycle.

Jacob gasped, wide-eyed. "But I didn't... that's the wrong gift!"

Molly put her hands on his shoulders. "No, son, it's yours. I know how much you wanted it, so Mr. Gilley made me a good offer on it. Now you can ride your route."

"And," Mr. Gilley turned to a helper who stood behind him carrying a large carton, "this is for you, Molly."

Molly covered her mouth, sucking in a breath as she saw the imprint on the box: Singer Electric Sewing Machine.

Jacob smiled and hugged her. "That's my gift to you, Mama."

Mr. Gilley wiped his eyes. "It appears the spirit of Christmas is alive and well. Merry Christmas!"

The Light Before Christmas

When our new neighbor introduced himself to us, his name should have been our first clue that life in our subdivision was about to get interesting. Edison Thomas seemed nice enough; he lived alone and kept pretty much to himself. Besides the name, nothing seemed odd at first.

Right after Halloween, I saw Edison stringing Christmas lights on the eaves of his house.

"Getting ready for the holidays?" I asked.

"You bet. I always like to get the lights out before it gets cold. You are going to be amazed at how this house shines when I'm done. My parents

didn't name me Edison for nothing. In fact, they said I was always attracted to light. The first word I uttered was 'yight.'" He laughed. This intriguing backstory was our second clue that something new was transpiring next door.

When the Indiana & Michigan Power Company truck appeared at his house the next day to do some major installation work, the third clue fell into place. We didn't want to pry, and we didn't have to; Edison proudly announced he needed more juice to power up his lights. We had always enjoyed Christmas lights, but we were beginning to wonder if Edison may have been related to or inspired by the Griswolds.

After that, every conversation we had with Edison seemed to revolve around Christmas lights. "Always was crazy about Christmas lights, ever since I saw my first C-6's as a child," he said.

"I loved changing bulbs and checking strings for burnouts. My daddy said I could smell a bad bulb a mile away. I still have a couple of cloth-covered strings of eight that I put on the dining room table. I drilled a special hole in the middle of the table and put an outlet in the floor, so Christmas dinner is always 'radiant.' I still have a few bubble lights too. Can't wait 'til Thanksgiving is over, so I can 'light up my life.' Yours too," he chuckled. The clues were mounting.

David's Landscaping arrived and planted several more evergreens and firs in Edison's yard. Soon, Edison was busy moving ladders and cords and plugs and setting up silhouetted creatures and figures all over his lawn. We didn't need any more clues. We knew: "The Light Before Christmas" was coming and would soon illuminate objects in Edison's yard—and ours—from the top of the porch to the top of the roof. And we couldn't just dash away. Still, we were intrigued with the whole production and wondered how it would look when he turned it on.

Thanksgiving leftovers had hardly been stored away when the telephone rang. Somehow I knew who it might be.

"Edison—it's you! Sure, we'll look out the window. Yes, it's going to be a great moment. O.K., we'll countdown with you… Five, four, three, two, one!"

The explosion of light that followed was unbelievable. We'd witnessed fireworks at Niagara and the lighting of Rockefeller Center at Christmas, but neither held a candle to Edison's display. My wife ran to get her sunglasses, while I considered getting the fire extinguisher, just in case.

"Whaddya think?" Edison's voice sparkled in my ear. "Ever seen anything like it?"

"Edison, I can truly say I never have."

"Well, enjoy it, neighbor, I'll only be giving this show every night through Christmas."

I had always wondered what it would be like to live in Alaska or anywhere far enough north that I would have to learn to sleep during daylight. Edison gave us a simulated opportunity. When word got around about his "Light Spectacular," the drive-bys began. Bumper-to-bumper traffic lined the roadway each night; Edison was so elated, he kept leaving the lights on later and later.

Greater than life-size outlines of Frosty, Santa, the Nativity, reindeer, toy soldiers, angels and gift boxes glittered and flashed; trees, shrubs, chimney, roof, windows, and even the porch swing sparkled. A huge fiber-optic sleigh ebbed and flowed with color. "Oohs" and "aahs" wafted from open car windows and drivers honked their horns in approval. Edison was ecstatic; we were mostly groggy.

"Lord," I prayed, "thank you for dormant grass in winter and for snow cover." My wife thought my prayer was silly until she realized too that tall, growing blades could be light-holding possibilities.

Christmas came and Edison took the lights down by New Year's Eve. We were glad he didn't want to celebrate the twelve days of Christmas with them.

21

After a dark and good night's sleep, we took sticky buns to Edison to wish him Happy New Year. He greeted us with a Christmas light catalog in hand.

"I'm ordering some terrific lights for next year. Look at this, it's called 'Dazzling Lawn Blanket.' Can't you just see it? It will be like having a light on every blade of grass."

So much for prayers. I called my earthly father as soon as we were back home.

"That's right, Dad, we want to spend Thanksgiving and Christmas with you next year. No, paying for plane tickets will be no problem. I just bought several shares of Indiana & Michigan Power and I'm expecting some great dividends, thanks to Edison Thomas. No, Dad, you heard his name right, but I do think there is a light connection to the inventor."

Belated Glad Tidings of Joy

*J*ohn Tyler turned the yellowed envelope over in his hand. In his many years as a postman, he had never seen anything like it. Brittle, peeling tuberculosis Christmas seals covered the back flap. Instead of a return address, the sender had simply written, "Joy to the World." The postmark was faded, but the month and year were discernible: December 1944. The card was as old as John.

He had found the card behind an old sorting bin at the post office. Presumably, the card had rested there until the bin was torn down fifty years after its initial construction. What intrigued him most was a hunch he had about the addressee, Miss Joy Pritchard.

Having lived in the small town of Elwood all his life, John knew practically everybody and their families. He guessed the card was meant for Lori Samson's mother, Joy, since Lori's middle name was "Pritchard," her mother's maiden name.

It makes sense, John thought as he drove to the old Pritchard residence. He and Lori had attended school together. He had never met her mother, but he had heard the stories about her. Joy was remembered as a rebellious teenager who ran off with a salesman. She became pregnant with Lori, and then the man abandoned her. Destitute and heartbroken, she returned to Elwood with Lori. Her widowed father forgave her and took them in to live with him.

Grief continued to befall the Pritchards over the years. Lori's grandfather died when she was ten, and Joy worked hard to raise her and send her to college. Lori married and, for a time, all seemed well. Then, Lori's husband died of a heart attack and Joy contracted a debilitating disease, so Lori returned to Elwood to care for her.

Perhaps the mysterious card will bring good news, he thought as he pulled into the driveway.

An elderly woman sat in a rocking chair on the porch. Taking a deep breath, John made his way up the walk. "Morning, Mr. Postman," the woman smiled. "Is this a special delivery?"

"Indeed it is, if you are… were Miss Joy Pritchard."

The smile faded. Her blue eyes opened wide, then narrowed. She leaned forward and squinted at the envelope.

"Is that a three-cent stamp?"

"Yes, ma'am. It appears to be a Christmas card. Are you Miss Pritchard?"

"Does it have a date on it?" Her mouth fell open and she sucked in a breath.

"Yes ma'am, December 1944. Now, if you're Miss Joy…"

"Oh, dear, oh, dear," she moaned. "He did send it!" She covered her face with her hands and rocked back and forth.

John need not ask again. He put one hand on her shoulder and placed the card in her lap. Her fingers touched the envelope and shook as they moved across it. She turned it over carefully, as if turning the reality of it over in her mind.

"Joy to the world," she whispered. "Would you open it?"

John slit the envelope open and handed it back. Her quivering fingers withdrew the card, and she clutched the long-lost treasure against her breast.

"Beloved Charlie. It's from my husband. I never thought I'd hear from him again."

John was full of questions, but he waited.

"Charlie and I eloped in 1944 after he was drafted because my father wouldn't sign papers for me to marry him. I became pregnant as Charlie was shipping out. He promised to send money so I could go to his grandmother's in Columbus and stay until he returned." She stopped to take a breath.

"Charlie was to put the money in a Christmas card so my father wouldn't suspect and write 'Joy to the World' as the return address. When I didn't get the card, I became desperate. A salesman offered to take me to Charlie's

27

grandmother's," she let out a moan, "but he didn't, he… oh, it was awful, too awful to tell."

Tears spilled down the crevices of her face. "After the baby came, he left me, and I came back home."

Her fingers trembled as she opened the card. She gasped as two twenty-dollar bills fell into her lap.

She closed her eyes and whimpered. "Oh, Charlie, you were faithful, and I wasn't."

"What happened to Charlie?"

"He was killed in the war. His family received the notice, but they never knew about us."

"I'm so sorry… Does your daughter know?"

"Oh, yes. I wanted her to know about her father. I can't wait until she gets home so I can show her this good news."

She bowed her head and whispered, "Thank you, Lord, for bringing glad tidings of Christmas from so long ago." She looked at John, "And thank you for bringing this precious card to me."

"It's my joy," John smiled, "and, it seems, for you too, Miss Pritchard."

At that Miss Pritchard burst into song, her squeaky soprano bringing life to the words on the envelope and the memories it held. John threw back his head and joined her in a rousing chorus of "Joy to the World."

Redeeming Christ in Christmas

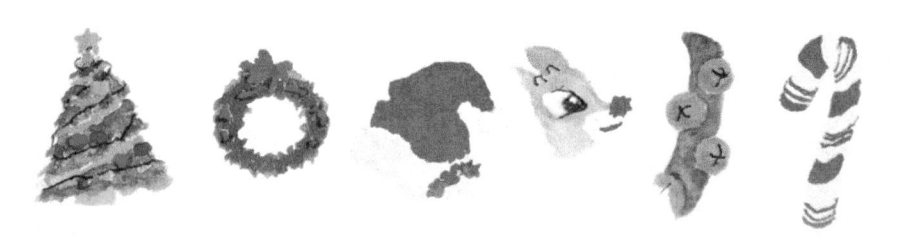

hat do Christmas trees, wreaths, Santa Claus, Rudolph, jingle bells, and candy canes have to do with the true meaning of Christmas?

These symbols, stories, and songs have been added over the years, and many of them appear to have no relevance to celebrating the birth of Christ. Almost all of us have spent many Christmases surrounded by these secular symbols; we either grew up in a "culturally correct" home that included them, or we chose to embrace the latest trends later in life. Sometimes we wonder if the reason for celebrating Christmas has been lost in a "secular shuffle."

Do we need to redeem Christmas? Should we discard all of the trimmings and trappings that have no relation to the first noel? Should we stop decorating trees and tell our children and grandchildren there is no Santa? Should we boycott watching Frosty and Rudolph videos and sing only carols that reference the nativity?

While there's nothing wrong with simplifying our Christmas traditions, what if, instead, we looked for opportunities to trace these cultural symbols, stories, and songs back to the first Christmas and its original meaning?

For example, the Christmas tree is a triangular shape, symbolic of the Trinity. It is evergreen, a symbol of eternal life in Christ. Its lights remind us that He is the light of the world. The ornaments can represent things Jesus did or things He created; ball ornaments, for instance, can remind us that God created the world, and that the gospel is given to the whole world. Garlands show how God wrapped His love around the whole world by sending His Son. A treetop star can represent the star that shone over Bethlehem as a guiding light to the shepherds and the wise men when Jesus was born.

Wreaths abound at Christmas. They represent a circle of love and can demonstrate the spiritual belief in life everlasting and the rebirth of the spirit. To Christians, they can be a way of professing the miracle birth of the Christ child.

We can tell our children and grandchildren the story of the real Santa Claus, who was originally named St. Nicholas and gave gifts to the poor, sometimes secretly. The Santas we see today can be said to represent what St. Nicholas started.

Rudolph lights the way for Santa, and we, as Christians, are to be the light of the world for Christ, even though we may be ridiculed like Rudolph. We need to be willing to shine a light of hope in this dark world, as Rudolph did.

Jingle bells were used on horses' harnesses to let others know the carriage was coming. Some were delightful sounds and others were annoying. Christians can make their presence known with loving and pleasant sounds in a cacophonous world. We can use our words to gain the attention of those who need to hear about Jesus.

Many stories abound about the origin of the candy cane. One tells about an Indiana candy maker who designed it to share the gospel. He fashioned the sweet peppermint delight out of hard rock candy to represent Christ as the solid rock, God's firm foundation. He shaped it into a staff to remind us of the Good

Shepherd. The staff turned upside down becomes a "J" for Jesus. White stripes symbolize the virgin birth and the sinless nature of Christ. Three small red stripes represent the scourging of Jesus on his way to the cross, and the single large red stripe reminds those with eyes to see and ears to hear how the blood Jesus shed paid for our sins. The candy maker shared the heart of Christmas and the gospel in one piece of candy! How sweet is that!

Ideas for sharing Christmas can be found in all the decorations we use, from the poinsettias that grace our tables to holly and mistletoe. We can use them to relate and tell the true Christmas story. They can be symbols that point to Christ as the center of our celebration and demonstrate how all that exists makes Christmas not just a "holi-day" but also a Holy Day.

We can "redeem" its sacred meaning by asking those who celebrate all its trappings if they know the Christ of Christmas. We can ask if they believe that God came down at Christmas so He could give them the first, best, and only lasting Christmas gift ever—forgiveness of their sins and eternal life with Him in heaven. We can share how accepting His gift of salvation through faith can change how they view Christmas. We can share what this gift means to us. If anyone hasn't accepted the gift of that first Christmas, then Christmas will simply be another chaotic cultural celebration, and its meaning will be bereft and unredeemed.

The Jesus Santa

Eddie stroked his white beard, grateful he didn't have to wear the fake one he had used 30 years before when he worked the Santa shift as a young man. Here he was again, same red suit, same mall. Providence had brought him back, and he was grateful for a job during tough times. The suit also fit better now without any padding, he noted, his own "bowlful of jelly" filling it.

The mall was a different story. The mall manager forbade him to share "The Real Meaning of Christmas" tracts as he had years before, and he was to spend no more than three minutes per child. After all, the manager told him, their parents needed to get to the stores to fulfill their child's wishes, didn't they?

"But it's Christmas," Eddie protested. "It's about Jesus."

"It's about business, Eddie, so stay on task here. Just be jolly and keep the line moving so the parents can shop. Would you rather go back to the Mission tent and tell about Jesus for nothing?"

Eddie capitulated, although he didn't feel jolly about it. He yearned to tell the children about Jesus. He loved sharing the Savior's story and the reason He came to earth, but now... it seemed a different message prevailed. The "scripted" words he was supposed to read were hollow. "Mind your parents. Happy Holidays. Ho ho ho."

Glancing at his watch, Eddie sighed—his shift was almost over. He looked up to see a pair of deep, piercing blue eyes, barely visible below a brow spilling over with golden curls. Before he could say "Ho ho ho," the girl climbed on his knee and demanded, "Are you the Jesus Santa?"

Eddie's own eyebrows rose in wonder. He looked over the girl's head for help from her mother, who was standing nearby. The woman simply gave a slight smile, shrugged, and looked down at her phone. The girl continued staring at him, waiting for an answer.

"What's your name, child?"

"Mary Katherine. I'm looking for the Jesus Santa. I've been waiting in line to see him."

"Why do you think I'm him?"

"My daddy told me. He said you told him about Jesus."

"Just what did he tell you?"

Mary Katherine folded her arms. "Jesus came from heaven to save us from our sins. He died on a cross and now He's in heaven with God. You know that. My daddy said Jesus sent you at Christmastime to tell people all about Jesus, so they could be saved. He said you told him when he was my age and he invited Jesus into his heart. You gave him a booklet about it. So, are you the Jesus Santa or not?"

"Well, Mary Katherine," Eddie started, then stopped. He spied the mall manager pointing to his watch and making "hurry-up" gestures. He recalled sharing the gospel with many children years ago, but dare he now?

Times change, but truth doesn't.

"Yes, child, I was—I am that Santa. I'll gladly share the story of Jesus, and if you haven't already, you can invite him into your heart too."

"I knew it was you!" Her golden curls intermingled with Eddie's beard as she clasped his neck. He squeezed his eyes shut and whispered a prayer. When he opened his eyes, he saw that the woman was also smiling through streams of tears. She stepped forward and took Eddie's hand.

"Thank you. This means so much."

"Are you Mary Katherine's mother?"

"Yes. You're an answer to prayer. You see, her father came to this same mall when he was Mary Katherine's age and met a man he called the 'Jesus Santa.' He told her she could come and meet him this year. But so many things have happened," her voice softened, and she lowered her eyes.

Eddie squeezed her hand. He could see the manager making his way to the platform.

Mary Katherine tugged his sleeve. "What happened was… Daddy went to heaven this year. He's with Jesus. His last wish was for me to meet the Jesus Santa."

The manager pushed in front of them, smiling at the people waiting in line. "Please stay where you are. Santa has to leave for a few minutes… uh, to check his lists." Leaning close to Eddie's ear, he whispered, "I warned you. You're fired!"

Eddie beamed at Mary Katherine and her mother. "Would you like to accompany me to the Mission tent where we can share the real Christmas story?" They glanced at the manager, looked at Eddie, and nodded.

Then Eddie turned to the people in line. "You've been waiting in line to see Santa, but if you follow us, you'll find a line to Jesus, where you can receive the best Christmas gift of all—eternal life."

Mary Katherine beamed as she took Eddie's hand in one of hers and her mother's in the other. "Yes! This is the Jesus Santa. Come and see!"

The Christmas We Missed Jesus

… for today in the city of David there has been born for you a Savior, who is Christ the Lord. This will be a sign for you: you will find a baby wrapped in cloths and lying in a manger. —Luke 2:11-12 NASB

Colored paper, boxes, and ribbon covered the living room floor, evidence that our family had lived up to the cultural expectations of Christmas. We were leaving on vacation the next day and needed to clear the debris, dismantle the tree, and pack away the decorations. Our oldest daughter was tasked with putting away the paper mâché figurines of Mary, Joseph, and the Christ child. Abruptly, she stopped and exclaimed in alarm, "I can't find baby Jesus." The baby was indeed missing from Mary's arms.

The search began. Everyone frantically pawed through wadded papers hoping to find the Christ child. Soon our youngest daughter shouted, "Here He is!" The precious figurine tumbled from some crumpled tissue. "Now He is safe, and we can put Him away until next year."

Later, after we had finished cleaning up and everyone had gone to bed, I stood looking out on newly fallen snow shimmering under a full moon and a starry sky of Christmas lights strung by God. I was suddenly overtaken by shame and remorse. How is it that we can celebrate Christmas so enthusiastically and yet miss it at the same time?

Busy with all the trappings—food, decorations, parties, and presents—we miss the main thing, the best part, the greatest gift: Jesus, the Christ child. Even when we do acknowledge Him as a decoration, we then proceed to pack Him away into the "Christmas closet" of our lives, intending to only bring Him out as a small figure in *our* celebration.

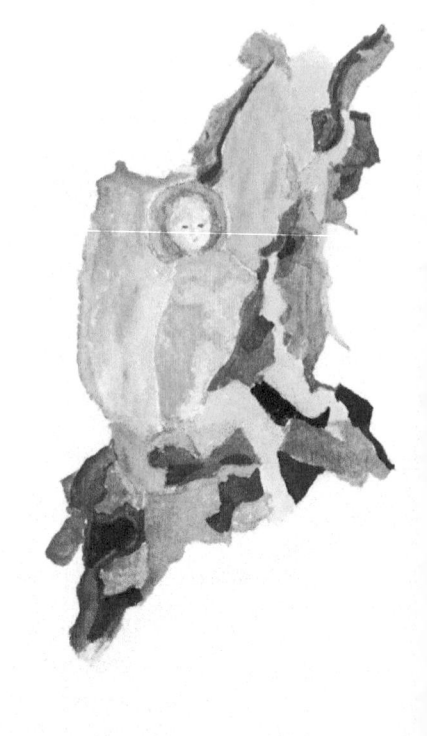

I cried as I prayed, *Father, forgive us for making ourselves the center of attention and forgetting Jesus. Thank you for showing us that without the gift of Your Son we are lost. May He have the prominence He deserves each day of the year, and especially at Christmas.*

Finding the missing figurine that year helped me find a new attitude toward celebrating Christmas. I treasure the lesson as God's gentle reminder: Without the Christ in Christmas in us, we have no true Christmas at all.

The Man Who Hated Christmas

arcus Smylie hated Christmas. He hated everything about it. He despised the commercials that interrupted his favorite shows and the music that played almost incessantly on his radio from October to December. But most of all, he detested it when anyone wished him "Merry Christmas." He even took wry pleasure in the fact that most people called him Marcus Scrooge behind his back.

Marcus hadn't always hated Christmas, especially during the many years he had shared it with Hattie. He was never as taken with it as she was, though. For her, it meant a relationship with God through His son Jesus, and Marcus didn't want a relationship with anyone but Hattie.

He liked the trappings of Christmas—the smell of pine as they trimmed the tree, the special Christmas cookies she baked, and the opportunity to shower her with gifts. She would say, "Oh, Marcus, you shouldn't have!" as she opened them, but he knew she was pleased, and pleasing Hattie was a joy to him. When he opened the gifts she gave him, he would say, "Thank you, but you are my Christmas gift, the most precious of all."

Then came the Christmas when he had lost his most precious gift. He thought it a cruel joke of God's for Hattie to die on Christmas Day. Marcus hated Christmas ever since.

Christmas was coming again, and the memory of Hattie's death with it. He chose to shut out the world and all its reminders, becoming a recluse in his house. He turned off the TV and radio, pulled down the shades, and kept only a small lamp lit so he could read.

One night as he sat reading, he drifted off and dreamed he saw Hattie hanging ornaments on the tree. The sound of her soprano voice was sweet as she sang "Joy to the World." He joined in. Then, suddenly, he heard a whole chorus singing the carol together. The voices grew. He bolted awake to realize the sound was real, and it was coming from outside.

He pulled back the curtain to see a group of carolers on his lawn, their faces shining from the candles they held as they sang, "Let heaven and nature sing." His heart quickened and his face flushed as he thrust open the front door.

"Stop that noise! Get off my lawn!"

Silence fell over the group as they stared in disbelief at the rebuff.

"Go on and sing your silly, meaningless songs somewhere else," Marcus barked.

As they turned to leave, a small girl looked back at him, her soft voice resonating in the night air. "Please, sir, we hope you have a Merry Christmas."

For a moment, he took in her candlelit face. Her eyes were pleading, stirring up a vision of another face pleading for him to know the Christ for whom Christmas was named.

"Not for me!" Marcus slammed the door on the face, the voice, and the memories.

"I'll have none of your Christmas," he shook his fist toward the ceiling. "Why would you take the most precious gift I ever had, and on the day she loved most? She never stopped talking about you or your son and how special it was for him to be born, but what good was it for her, for anyone?"

Sleep did not come easily for Marcus that night as he kept seeing the child's face in the darkness. Her voice reminded him of Hattie's entreaties that she would repeat every year: "Jesus came to save you too, Marcus. Christmas isn't really Christmas for you until you receive Him."

The next morning as he stooped to pick up his newspaper from the front porch. Marcus found a small package, wrapped in crinkled Christmas paper and tied with twine. He opened it to find six decorated Christmas cookies on a paper plate. Underneath was a piece of paper with chunky crayon-printed words: "I made these for Santa, but I thought you might like some too. Love, Sophie."

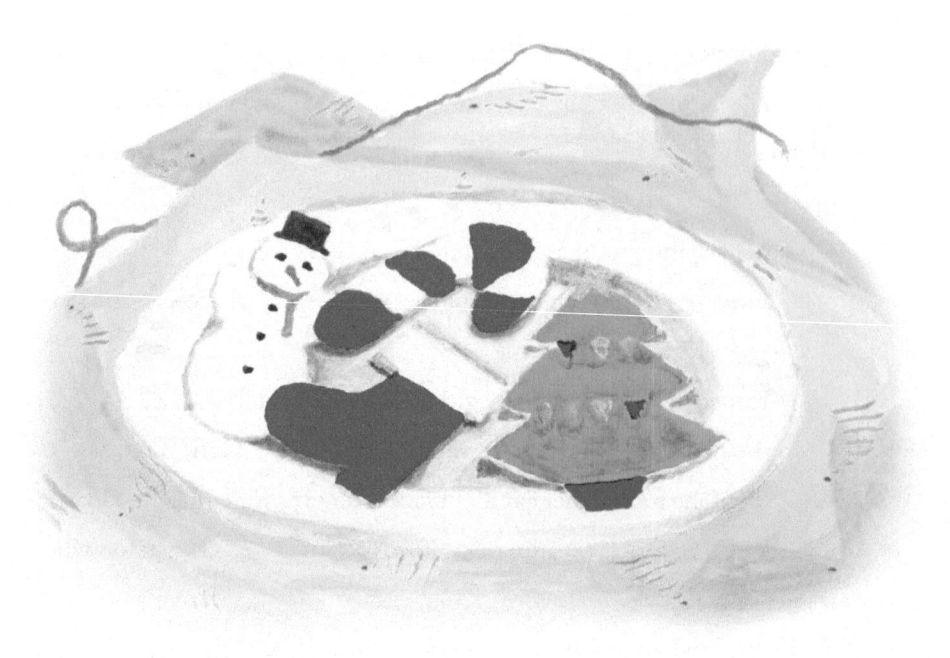

Maybe it's a joke. Maybe they're poisoned. He couldn't resist, so he took them inside and bit into one. The soft sweetness melted on his tongue. *Tastes just like Hattie's.* He ate another, and as he savored the treat, he felt a warmth he hadn't felt in a long time. He wondered who this Sophie was.

The ringing of the doorbell commanded his attention and, with the plate still in hand, he opened the door to find a short, bundled figure holding a steaming cup. Auburn curls peeked out from a knitted cap and rimmed the face of a rosy-cheeked girl. He recognized her as the small caroler.

Her frosty breath blew words at him. "Hi, mister. I'm Sophie. I see you found my cookies. My Grams taught me how to bake them. I wanted you to have some hot chocolate to go with them. Would you hold it, please, while I stomp my feet?"

She thrust the cup into his hand without waiting for an answer. Marcus simply stared as she stomped the snow off her boots and slid past him into the room. "I hope you have a fire going; it's really cold out."

"I don't have a fire."

"Well, I can show you how to start one. My Grams taught me. Hey, where's your Christmas tree?"

"I don't have a tree."

"I kinda guessed that. Sorry." She squinted at him. "Is it really true that you hate Christmas?"

"It's true. I don't like it."

"I know how that feels. I used to hate Christmas too."

Marcus almost smiled to hear this revelation from one so young.

"Go ahead and drink the chocolate before it gets cold. I already had some and it's extra good. My Grams…"

"Taught you how to make it," Marcus finished the sentence as he took a sip. "It's good."

"Yes sir. She's taught me a lot of things. She taught me not to hate Christmas too."

"Really?" Marcus squinted at her and cocked his head.

"Really." Sophie took off her coat and sat in Marcus's chair. "I hated it because of what happened. Do you want to hear about it?"

"I think you're going to tell me."

"It happened three years ago. My momma and daddy and I had gone to church for the Christmas Eve service, and we were heading home. The roads were snow covered and icy, but Daddy was a good driver, so I wasn't worried. We were singing a Christmas song—actually, we sang it to you last night: 'Joy to the World.'" She stopped and took a breath.

"Well, we were singing it when suddenly, there were these bright lights coming right toward us. Momma screamed and I covered my face. The next thing I knew, there was a loud crash and my body lunged forward, my head hit something hard, and then everything went black. When I woke up, I was in the hospital with all kinds of tubes in me. Machines were making noises and a nurse was saying I was okay. I was alive."

Sophie rolled her lips together and squeezed her eyes shut, as if she wanted the story to end there. Marcus wanted it to end too because he perceived what might be coming.

She sighed. "Then they told me. Momma and Daddy didn't make it." Tears spilled with the words. "I'm sorry. It still hurts to remember."

Marcus's eyes burned and welled up. His anger had been the only part of himself that he allowed to burn until this moment. Now, for the first time in years, he felt something else, a stirring in his heart. He knelt beside the girl and touched her shoulder. "I'm sorry, Sophie."

She wiped her eyes and patted his hand. "It's okay, Mister Marcus. I'm okay, now. I miss them still. And I was like you—I hated Christmas. I couldn't understand why my parents had to die, and especially then. But Grams told me what Christmas is all about. Do you know the whole story?"

"Well, I know Christmas is about Jesus' birth and many people still worship him as a god."

"He's not just *a* god. God sent Jesus to save us from our sins. Grams explained how when I told a lie or wished something bad would happen to someone, that was a sin."

"I can't imagine you wishing someone ill."

"Well, I used to wish Bobby Taylor would trip and smash his nose. He was always pushing people and tripping them. But now I just pray he'll change and stop that kind of stuff. I always felt kinda guilty for thinking bad things like that.

Grams said that God was showing me that I needed to be forgiven and the only way to do that was to pay for my sins. Since I couldn't, she explained that Jesus did because He lived a perfect life. He died so God would forgive me. And the best part is that He didn't stay dead; He rose from the dead. It's all in the Bible. Do you have a Bible?"

"No, I don't."

"I have one. I could lend it to you. You could read how Jesus died and went to heaven and if we believe in him, we will go there too. That's where my momma and daddy are now. And that's why I don't hate Christmas anymore, and maybe you wouldn't either, if you'd read the whole story."

"Maybe."

"Can I ask you something, Mister Marcus? It's kinda personal."

"You can ask, Sophie."

"I know Mrs. Smylie died, and I'm sorry. Grams told me. She said Mrs. Smylie knew the story about Jesus and believed in Him, so she must be in heaven with my parents too, right?"

Marcus turned away. His eyes fell on Hattie's picture on the desk and on the object beside it. The leather book lay untouched, although he had promised her that he would read it.

"I'm sorry, Mister Marcus. Maybe I shouldn't have asked, but here's the thing. When I die, I'm going to heaven and I will see my momma and daddy again. When you die, if you don't go to heaven, Mrs. Smylie is going to miss you."

"You really believe that, don't you? I'm not sure..." Marcus picked up Hattie's Bible from the desk.

"Is that a Bible? I thought you said you didn't have one."

"I don't. It was Mrs. Smylie's."

"Well, if you read it, you'll see how much God loves you and what Jesus did for you."

"I don't know where to start."

"Here, let me show you." Sophie opened the Bible and turned to the book of John. "Read all of John's book and you'll get the message."

"I'll think about it."

"I hope you will. Gosh, I didn't realize what time it is. I need to go home before Grams comes looking for me."

Sophie donned her coat and gave Marcus a quick hug. "I really hope you will have a Merry Christmas, Mister Marcus."

Marcus smiled. "Perhaps. Thank you, Sophie, for the cookies, the chocolate… and for sharing your story with me."

Later, the Bible lay open on Marcus's lap. His fingers rested on John chapter 3 with verse 16 highlighted and the word "world" marked through. Above it in Hattie's handwriting was his name. He closed his eyes as tears streamed down his face. He whispered a prayer to God, Hattie's God.

"I want to know You, LORD. Forgive me for keeping You out of my life. I want the joy that Hattie knew and Sophie has. Please save me, Jesus, so I might be with You and Hattie someday. And thank you for sending Sophie to me."

That night he slept well, and a new dream came. The sound of voices singing "Joy to the World" wafted through the air. He saw the faces of the choir and he recognized one whose face was all aglow. She stopped singing. Her eyes glistened as she nodded and smiled. Her lips moved and he read the words they formed: "Oh, Marcus!"

Special Delivery Christmas

Luke cupped his hands over his mouth and blew into them, then rubbed his palms together. He reckoned this was the coldest winter he had known in all his eleven years—at least that he could remember.

It had also been a hard winter so far. Papa had been gone a week now, leaving Luke in charge.

"I'll be back by Christmas Day," Papa had told him and Lydia, Luke's mother. "You know if you need to, you can call Dr. Evans and he will come right away. I wish I didn't have to go, but a promise made is a promise kept."

Lydia had smiled and put one arm around Luke and the other across her protruding belly, giving it a pat. "We'll be fine. We have a couple more weeks before the baby is due."

Luke stood up a little taller. "I'll take care of everything, Papa. Don't worry."

He was determined to keep that promise. He assumed all the chores of feeding chickens, milking Bessie and feeding her calf, keeping the wood stove stoked, and helping Mama stay calm. Luke wanted to show Papa he could handle whatever might come.

Luke put his gloves on and picked up the milk buckets, still steaming from Bessie's contribution. He sidled past the Ford pickup Papa had pulled into the barn before he left to keep it out of possible bad weather. Papa had been wise, as always, because a storm had descended on Christmas Eve, and drifts were mounding all around the farmyard.

Luke pushed the barn door shut as gusts of snow pelted his face. He set the buckets down and pulled his scarf around his head. He sighed, picked up the pails, and plodded on through the snow-drifted path towards the house. The lights on the Christmas tree in the front window shone like a multi-colored beacon leading him to safety and warmth. Snowflakes stung his eyes as he blinked. "One more day," he said aloud. Tomorrow was Christmas, and Papa would be home.

Luke entered the house to the welcoming warmth of the fire he had stoked earlier. His mother sat in her rocker, wrapped up in an afghan, her Bible propped open on her stomach.

"Oh, son, how cold you must be!" Lydia laid the book aside and started to rise.

"Stay put, Mama. I'm fine." Luke peeled off his boots and shed his coat and scarf. He took the milk pails to the kitchen where he strained them and bottled the contents for storage in the refrigerator.

"Come sit so we can read the Christmas story," Lydia called when he had finished.

Luke sat down on the couch near her, and she began to read from the family Bible. Reading the story from the gospel of Luke was a Christmas Eve tradition.

"And she gave birth to her newborn son..." The sound of the telephone ringing interrupted her story. Luke jumped up to answer it, then handed it to his mother.

He could hear the familiar voice on the other end of the line and knew what was happening before Lydia said a word. Papa was calling to say he would not make it home for Christmas because the storm had delayed the train. He said he was happy the call even went through, since the storm had downed some phone lines. Lydia assured him all was well and that Luke had everything under control. They would look for him on the 26th.

Lydia hung up the phone, sighed, and looked away, squeezing her eyes shut out of Luke's view.

"It's okay, Mama. We want him to be safe. Keep reading the story."

She turned back to him and smiled. "It's just one more day. We'll wait 'til he gets home to celebrate. That will be our Christmas gift."

Christmas morning came with sunshine glistening on the snowdrifts and making icicles form like daggers dangling from the eaves of the porch. Luke broke one off and licked it as he went to the barn to do his chores. He slid the large door open and shimmied past the truck to Bessie's stall. After completing his chores, he headed back to the house saying the same three words to himself: "One more day."

Then he heard the sound, the shrill, cascading cry. At first he thought it was the barn cat's hungry howl, but he had just left some fresh milk for it. The cry grew louder as he neared the house. He dropped the buckets and ran inside. His mother was lying in her bed, moaning, her legs drawn up. A strong ammonia-like odor filled the air. She waved her hand at him to stop.

"The baby's coming! Call Dr. Evans!"

Luke ran to the phone and picked up the receiver to dial, but there was no dial tone. He pushed down again. Nothing. The line must be down.

He went to the bedroom and took his mother's hand. The pains had subsided, and she was breathing more slowly. He told her his plan.

"I can do it, Mama. I have to. Just ask God to help you hang on until I get back."

She looked into his steel blue eyes and placed her hand on his curly head. "Oh, son. Please be careful."

When Dr. Evans saw the Ford pickup pull into his driveway—braking hard and horn honking—his mouth flew open. The truck appeared as if it was driving itself. Then Luke spilled out of it and called to him, "The baby's coming!" The doctor grabbed his bag and told Luke to leave the truck. They scrambled into the doctor's car and sped back to the farmhouse.

They arrived to find Luke's mother grunting and writhing with contractions. Dr. Evans spat orders at Luke. "Can you do what I tell you, son?"

"Yes sir! I helped with Bessie when she calved."

A little while later, a new cry filled the room and a wrinkled, red-streaked form with flailing arms and legs made its debut. Dr. Evans lifted the baby up and smiled. "Merry Christmas, Lydia, you have a daughter. And Luke, you have a sister!" He wrapped the baby in a blanket and placed her in Lydia's arms. Lydia's brow was wet with sweat, her cheeks streaming with tears of joy.

"Thank you, Lord, for sending this child to bless us today on Christmas, just as we're celebrating the birth of Jesus who came to us long ago."

The next day Dr. Evans drove the Ford pickup to the train station to pick up Papa and bring him and the truck home. When Papa asked him why he was driving his truck, the doctor told him the whole story. Papa kept saying, "Oh, my!" Then he laughed and said, "That's my boy!" He thanked God that all had gone well and Mama and baby were healthy.

In the end, Luke judged it was the best Christmas he had seen in all his eleven years. Luke's parents named the baby Mary Christina, since she was born on Christmas, and they praised Luke for fetching the doctor and helping with the delivery. Luke said he didn't do anything special; he simply did what he saw his father do. Papa said that if he always followed in the steps of his heavenly Father, he would be a fine man.

O Christmas Tree

The smell of pine fills up the room, emitting from the tree,
standing bare in stanchion tall.
"It's Christmas time," I say.

I untangle strings of bulbs and thread them through the limbs—
crystal-white, like sprinkled stars
shining still today.

I unwrap the angel fair and place her at the top.
She's like the ones who spoke glad news
on that first Christmas day.

I bring forth the ornaments, treasures kept in store.
A creche made of fine porcelain,
it's message to display.

I hang birds and flowers, created by God's hand,
then painted hearts with printed names
molded out of clay.

I place a resin Santa, kneeling by the babe,
and next to it a wooden cross
that He would bear someday.

I wrap the tree with garland, stark red against the green,
like drops of blood of His who died
for us who'd gone astray.

O Christmas tree so lovely, such joy you bring to me!
Each year I celebrate with you
this blessed Holy Day.

Tina's Blessing Carol

The man dressed as Santa stood by the red pot, ringing a bell in front of the Five and Dime—"Help the needy—share the Christmas spirit!" Most people responded by pulling coat collars up over their ears and diverting their eyes to the slush below. They didn't want to admit that many of them were recipients of help from the kettle. The dark clouds of the Great Depression hung over us, obscuring any spirit of Christmas.

Momma dropped my hand long enough to scavenge some coins from her purse and drop them in the kettle. "Bless you, ma'am," Santa said.

I tugged Momma's sleeve in protest. "Momma! Why are you giving money away? We won't have enough for our own Christmas."

Momma stooped down to match my ten-year-old stature, her blue eyes capturing mine with that "teachable moment" stare I knew all too well.

"Christmas is about blessing, child. God blessed us with the gift of His son, and we're to bless others by sharing what we have that they don't. Everyone has a blessing to share."

I tucked the message in the back of my mind, thinking I would understand it when I grew up, but Tina Carver was to prove me wrong. Tina was in my class at school, and her family was on the charity list. Her father had hopped a freight to parts unknown when he lost his job, leaving her, her mother, and her two brothers to scrape by any way they could. They lived in an abandoned storefront near the tracks, its shattered windows covered by cardboard.

Some of the kids made fun of Tina. She wore her brother's hand-me-down coats and trousers to school, making her stand out starkly from the rest of us girls, who wore dresses and leggings. Most times her clothes and hands were smudged with coal dust from picking up pieces along the tracks to feed their potbelly stove.

Momma's "compassion" lesson began to take root when I donned a pair of my brother's old pants and wore them to school to support Tina. The kids didn't laugh, but Tina did. I knew then I'd found a new friend, so I offered to share lunch with her.

"I don't have anything to give you."

"Don't have to. It's a blessing. God blessed me with extra cornmeal mush so I could share." But even as I shared my blessing, I began to wonder, *What blessing did Tina have to share?*

We walked home together. As I helped Tina pick up coal and tuck the pieces into an old knapsack, I began humming a Christmas carol. Suddenly, the voice of an angel burst forth, singing the words in perfect soprano.

I was dumbstruck. "Tina! Where did you learn to sing like that?"

Tina stopped. "Sorry. Never sung around nobody but my mom. Didn't mean to hurt your ears."

"My ears are fine and so is your voice—it's beautiful! Tina, you have to sing in the school Christmas program."

"Can't."

"Why not?"

"Uh... I don't have a dress to wear."

"No problem. I have one I outgrew. It's just your size."

The Christmas program was the same every year—classes crowded onto the gym stage and sang carols chosen by the music teacher, Miss Morgan. Parents applauded politely to the cacophony of voices until the final carol, "Silent Night," brought relief.

However, when we all filed into the auditorium to perform, we instantly discovered that this year was going to be different, *very* different.

Miss Morgan showed up with laryngitis, so Principal Hanley had to introduce the songs. Then we discovered Mr. Shricker, the janitor, had left a window open to air out the gym and cold moisture had thrown the piano out of tune.

"We'll just have to sing acapella," Miss Morgan whispered as she ushered the first graders onto the stage.

"I thought we were thinging 'Away in the Manger,'" Willie Morgan lisped.

"We are, Willie, but we need someone to start us."

Tina stood beside me behind the curtain as we waited for our turn. I pushed her onto the stage. "Go! You can start us!"

A hush fell over the room as everyone stared.

"Tina?" Miss Morgan rasped in surprise.

Tina fumbled with the lace trim on my hand-me-down dress and looked out over the audience. Her eyes met those of her mother, who smiled and nodded. Tina took a deep breath.

The next sound out of her mouth came straight from heaven. Tina's melodic voice swept through the gym, singing the carol as we had never heard it sung. "Away in a Manger," a humble message from a humble messenger in perfect pitch, resonated sweet tones of hope to hungry souls. The children joined in, and the audience applauded.

Tina's gift proved Momma right—everyone does have a blessing to share.

I'll Be Home for Christmas

Kevin sat waiting for Marcy by the mall fountain, watching the moving mosaic of shoppers and listening to strains of Christmas songs drifting from the loud speaker. The dancing waters mesmerized him. *I never knew shopping could be so exhausting. But then, Annie always did it for me.*

"Daddy, Daddy, look!" Kevin's heart skipped a beat as he turned toward the familiar-sounding voice of a child. *Missy?* Instead of seeing corn-silk curls coiling around the rosy cheeks he had touched so many times, he beheld a pint-sized brunette tugging on her father's sleeve. A twinge of envy struck him. *Oh, how I wish it were you, Missy! If only…*

"Kev, babe, you doin' okay?" Not waiting for an answer, Marcy handed him three shopping bags, then leaned over and kissed him. "You're my best Christmas gift this year," she winked. "Just have a couple more to get… Be back in a jif."

Strains of Perry Como crooning "I'll Be Home for Christmas" wafted over the sound system to oblivious shoppers, but the lyrics penetrated Kevin's thoughts. *Home… Where is home this year?*

He closed his eyes, and a memory thrust itself forth. He saw Annie and Missy in the kitchen making Christmas cutouts. Missy, cheeks aglow with excitement and smears of red icing, stood on a stool waving a spatula. "Look, Daddy, we're making cookies for Santa…"

What had he said? Something like, "That's nice" or, "I don't have time for Santa or Christmas cookies." Last Christmas was a fog. So much had happened since then. The ugly arguments were ended only by a wall of silence on Annie's part or by his storming out the door and spending less and less time at home.

His eyes drifted to the fountain again. The streams of water exploded into tall designs of individual droplets, cascading into the sea of water below. *That's how it was with Annie and me, our actions and words erupting until we were consumed by the prevailing waters of the times when it was easy to just go with the flow of people getting divorced.* Eventually he had succumbed to the echoing voices—"If you're not happy, just get out. There's plenty of women out there eager to please."

It was true. Shortly after they separated and he moved out, Marcy appeared—young, bubbly, vivacious, smothering him with attention. She was all too eager to keep him from thinking he had failed, particularly as a father to Missy.

"She'll be fine," cooed Marcy. "Kids adjust. Besides, you're free to spend time with little ol' me."

At first he had felt free; he needn't hurry home after work, could sleep in if he wanted on weekends, and follow all his fantasy sports teams without reproach. As Christmas approached, however, something kept gnawing at him, a restlessness that he couldn't seem to suppress.

The words of another familiar song broke the reverie. Bing Crosby was dreaming of a "White Christmas," as he had done for decades before Kevin was born. *Is every song about dreams? Is life only filled with disappearing visions like the mist in the fountain?* He had dreamed of having a family of his own, a place to call home, and now…

A gritty unshaven man dressed in a stocking cap, mismatched clothing and tattered tennis shoes caught Kevin's attention. The man stooped under a bulging, threadbare backpack as he shuffled from one trash can to another, rummaging for discarded aluminum cans or other treasures to add to the plastic garbage bag he dragged along.

Poor homeless soul. The lightning thought pierced Kevin's consciousness and his eyes stung. *That's me! Homeless.* He tried to swallow, but the yearning would not yield this time. *Oh, God, what have I done? Is it too late?*

"Here I am, sugar. Sorry about the wait," Marcy bubbled. "Hey, Kev, you catchin' a cold or somethin'?"

"We need to talk, Marcy…"

*

Kevin punched the speed-dial number on his cell, took a deep breath, and prayed. *Please, Lord, give me another chance.*

"Wilsons' residence." Annie's greeting warmed and surprised him all at the same time.

"Hello? Anyone there?" she said when he didn't respond right away.

"Annie. It's me. I was wondering… uh… how you and Missy are doing."

He waited, knowing Annie would be weighing her response.

"We're doing okay… how about you?"

"I'm doing okay too."

"That's good. Would you like to speak to Missy?"

"Yes. No, I mean, not yet. I want to talk to you." He took a deep breath. "Annie, I lied, I'm not okay—I'm miserable. I was wondering… Annie, I'm so sorry about everything." He waited for a response. "Annie? Are you there?"

"Yes, I'm here." Those three simple words, soft and tender, gave him a glimmer of hope.

"You were wondering?" she prompted after a minute, her voice almost a whisper.

"I was wondering if you could forgive me… if we could try to… if I…" He choked. "I want to come home." There it was, all the longing of his heart spilled out and laid bare.

"Is that Daddy?" He closed his eyes at the faint sound of Missy's voice.

"Yes, he…" He heard Annie speak, but he couldn't make out the words.

"Annie? Did you hear me?"

A squeal came through the line in the background. "Daddy, it's you! Are you coming home? Oh, please come home! We want you to!"

"Annie, do you want me to?" He closed his eyes again and prayed.

"Can you be home for Christmas?" Her words made him shiver.

"Can I? Yes, yes, absolutely! I'll be home. You can count on me."

The Christmas Gift that Wasn't

For it is by grace you have been saved, through faith—and this is not from yourselves, it is the gift of God. —Ephesians 2:8 (NIV)

The popular cultural tradition of giving gifts at Christmas is, in many cases, merely an exchange. We give gifts to others because they give gifts to us. Often the exchange is out of obligation, or a belief that the gift is expected. We might give gifts to impress others or to elicit gratitude or favors from them in return. This kind of "gift" is really a trade transaction, rather than authentic gift-giving. By definition, a true gift is "something willingly given to someone without payment; a present." When we give something to someone who cannot give us anything in return, or we give without expecting a reward, *that's* a genuine gift.

A good example of this type of giving was a "Secret Santa" millionaire who for years gave out $100 bills to strangers at Christmastime. As a result, others have followed his example, and charitable organizations have started with variations of "Secret Santa" in their name.

Receiving a gift with no strings attached is a wonderful experience, and that's exactly what God did for the whole world. On that first Christmas centuries ago, God gave us a gift when He sent Jesus, His son, to be born in human form to redeem us. His death on the cross as an atoning sacrifice was a completely unmerited gift. His shed blood is payment for all our sins, freeing us from condemnation and God's judgment. His resurrection, which conquered death and opened the way to eternal life, is a gift to all who believe and receive Him.

God did all this in one amazing gift of grace with no strings attached. We did nothing to earn or deserve this gift, nor are we expected to give anything back in exchange. "For the wages of sin is death, but the free gift of God is eternal life in Christ Jesus our Lord." Romans 6:23 (NASB)

And, if that wasn't enough, God gives us His Spirit as an ongoing gift that imparts new mercies to us every day, just as Jesus promised: "But the Helper, the Holy Spirit, whom the Father will send in my name, he will teach you all things and bring to your remembrance all that I have said to you." John 14:26 (ESV)

"Thanks be to God for his indescribable gift!" 2 Cor 9:15 (NIV)

Heavenly Father, we offer our humble gratitude for Your gift to us—Christ, our Savior and Lord.

The Christmas Suit

I n his mind, Barney Cooper thought he was clever—and lucky too. He had found an insulated thermos someone had discarded in the trash barrel at the park. He washed it out at the nearby water fountain, looking around to make sure no one was watching. Then, he pulled the whiskey bottle out of his pocket and carefully poured its contents into the thermos, stuffing the empty bottle down into the trash barrel. He took a swig from the bottle and smiled at his good fortune.

He pulled his coat collar up against the December wind, but he was warm inside. A lady came walking by with her dog. He tipped his cap and held the thermos up as if to toast her. "Sure is nice to have hot coffee on a cold day like this, huh?"

The woman turned, yanking on her dog's leash as she quickened her pace away from him. Barney held the thermos up to her back and sneered, "Merry Christmas to you too!"

Barney moved on, trying to savor his drink because he knew he had no money left to buy more. He hoped he could get a handout from one of the churches he hadn't hit yet. He knew Christmas time was good for appealing to Christian compassion. He chuckled and murmured to himself, "Those religious folks are the best. They empty their pockets so easily when I give them a sob story."

Yes, Barney Cooper thought he was very clever and lucky until he met Pastor Willie Thompson of the Cornerstone Christian Church.

Pastor Willie had known hard times himself. He was the son of a single mother and had worked his way through college. "God called me into ministry and called me to Cornerstone Christian to preach the gospel," he told people.

Cornerstone Christian was mostly made up of poor farming families, except for Thomas Booker, a banker whose grandfather had founded the church. His offerings were substantial, while most of the donations from the other congregants were meager at best. Many a time the poorer families gave to Pastor Willie in kind—chickens or eggs or vegetables.

"Thank you for your blessing," he'd say. "My table thanks you and my stomach is grateful."

Thomas Booker not only tithed in cash but gave other gifts of value to the church and to Pastor Willie. He maintained the upkeep of the church and parsonage and provided a car for Willie. He took pride in being able to keep the church going and see to the pastor's care.

One day, Thomas noticed Pastor Willie wore the same black suit each week. It was shopworn—the lapels were shiny and the cuffs and collar were fraying. With Christmas coming, Thomas had his tailor make a dark blue three-piece suit for Pastor Willie. The only condition was that Willie wear it for the Christmas service.

"Oh my," Willie blushed. "You are so kind. I'm grateful, Thomas, but do you think folks will recognize me in it?"

Thomas smiled. "It's my pleasure to give what I can in appreciation for your service to us at Cornerstone."

Not long after the suit arrived from the tailor's, Barney Cooper decided to seek out the pastor of Cornerstone Christian Church for a handout. He had run out of money and made his way to the parsonage. He rang the doorbell and stood with cap in hand, head hanging down.

When Pastor Willie opened the door, Barney made sure not to look him in the eye. He shifted his feet and cleared his throat. "Good day, Pastor. I've heard how you preach the good news and I'm truly in need of some." He paused, waiting to see how Willie would react.

"Come inside, sir. Don't stand in the cold."

Barney wiped his feet on the doormat and stepped into the warmth of the parsonage. "Thank you for your kindness. May you be blessed."

"How can I help you?"

"Well, you see, Pastor, I was hurt in an accident, injured my back, and lost my job." He frowned and placed one hand on his back.

"I'm sorry. Do you need medical care?"

Barney chuckled and shook his head. "Oh no, sir. The thing is, I recovered." He took a couple of steps back and forth to show his agility. "And now, I have this opportunity to get a new job and I have an interview scheduled today." He paused.

"How can I help?"

"Well, as you can see, my clothes are, well, not the best for an interview. But there's a thrift shop downtown where I could buy some things, if... I had some funds to do so." He lowered his eyes.

"I see." Pastor Willie stroked his chin and sized Barney up. "I don't have funds to give you, but I may have something better."

He went to the closet and pulled out the blue serge suit. "This may be just your size."

Barney's eyes widened at the sight of the suit. He started calculating how much money he could get for it and could almost taste the whiskey in his throat. He hung his head and wiped his eyes.

"Oh, good pastor," Barney spoke in broken tones. "You don't know what this means for me. Your compassion will be rewarded in heaven."

After Barney donned the suit, he asked, "How do I look?"

Pastor Willie noticed how well Barney filled the suit. Then he noticed the man's raggedy shoes.

"You need one more thing." Pastor Willie brought out a pair of shoes that he kept safely in the closet. He only donned them for special church events. "These will make you shine."

Barney put on the shoes and pumped Pastor Willie's hand as he turned to leave. "I know I'll do well now, thanks to you. As they say, 'clothes make the man.'"

"Wait. You're not quite ready." Willie went to the kitchen, returned with a towel, and knelt in front of Barney. "The shoes are dusty. Let me polish them up for you."

Barney could not speak. He shook Willie's hand again and hurried out the door before the pastor could offer to do anything else.

The night of the Cornerstone Christmas service found Pastor Willie giving the sermon wearing his old black suit. No one noticed except Thomas Booker, who squirmed in his pew and couldn't wait to ask what had happened.

As was the custom in all his sermons, but especially at Christmastime, Pastor Willie preached the gospel.

"God sent His Son Jesus at Christmas as a child, but He came to die on a cross for our sins. He was buried and rose again. If you believe in Christ and accept His gift of salvation, you will have eternal life too. All you must do is confess your sin and ask Jesus to save you. Is there anyone here who would like to receive this special Christmas gift?"

"I would," a man's voice rang out from the back of the church. He stood, stepped into the aisle, and walked to the altar. He was impeccably dressed in a dark blue suit.

Thomas Booker gasped when he recognized the suit he had bought for Pastor Willie. Pastor Willie reached out to shake Barney Cooper's hand.

"Welcome, Barney."

"Can I say something?"

Pastor Willie nodded.

Barney turned to face the congregation and cleared his throat. "My name is Barney Cooper and I am a sinner." He stopped and took a breath. "I went to your pastor to get money or something I could sell for money so I could buy whiskey." He stopped again and sniffed. "I lied to him about wanting the money to get suitable clothes for a job interview, and he gave me this new suit." He brushed his hand down the front of it. "I figured I could sell it to the second-hand store for money."

Barney wiped his eyes and choked. "But your pastor did something that broke my heart. He gave me this pair of shoes, and he knelt down before me and shined them. I could not believe someone would care that much about me. After hearing the sermon, I know why."

He fell to his knees before Pastor Willie, sobbing. "Please forgive me. I don't deserve these clothes. I don't deserve your kindness. I didn't sell them and I'm not drinking anymore. I know I need help. I know I need Jesus so I can be a man like you."

Pastor Willie placed his hand under Barney's chin and lifted it so their eyes met. He smiled and helped him to his feet. "Jesus will give you what you need,

Barney, and He will help you become a man dressed in His righteousness so you can be like Him." He turned to the congregation, "Amen?"

The people stood, including Thomas Booker, applauding and shouting a hearty "Amen!"

The Tree Nobody Wanted

Miss Beulah held tight the smaller hand in hers, taking short steps to match Dorie's labored ones. Even with the leg braces, Dorie had a hard time navigating the crushed stone pathway at the Christmas tree lot.

"Looking for the perfect tree for the Chapel Christmas?" Miss Beulah and Dorie stopped and turned towards the sound of the voice. It was Mr. Wilkins, who owned the lot.

Miss Beulah smiled. "Yes, indeed. This is Dorie Lambert, who will be making the selection this year."

"Well, Miss Dorie, congratulations on being selected to pick the Chapel's tree. You join a nice tradition of middle-schoolers from Miss Beulah's Sunday school class."

"Thank you. I'm excited to do it."

"She deserves it. She memorized the most verses in my class." Miss Beulah put her arm on Dorie's shoulder and gave her a squeeze.

"We have some fine trees from which to choose—pine, spruce, and fir. Most have great shapes, are nice and tall, and have thick branches. Make your pick and I'll load it for you."

PAY HERE

Miss Beulah and Dorie made their way through the lot, examining the possibilities. Some were tall and slim with short, prickly needles, while others spread their limbs in a broad array as if they had feathers.

"What do you think, Dorie? Do you see a favorite?"

Dorie shook her head. She glanced over the orderly rows again, then noticed several trees leaning against the checkout stand. Some were thin and raggedy; some had broken limbs.

She walked over and took a closer look. She pointed to one of the trees. "This is it. I want this one."

"That tree isn't for sale," Mr. Wilkins said as he came up behind her. "It's a reject. See how it's shaped? Nobody wants a tree like that."

Dorie looked at Miss Beulah, then looked down and whispered, "I want it."

Miss Beulah cocked her head, raised her brows, and caught Mr. Wilkins' eye. "Maybe Dorie sees something in the tree we don't."

Dorie took hold of the main trunk and looked at Mr. Wilkins. "See the trunk and the main branch going across it?"

Mr. Wilkins put his hands on his hips and frowned. "Yes. That's what makes it so unattractive. They are both too big, and there aren't enough small branches with needles to cover them."

Dorie tugged Miss Beulah's sleeve and said, "It's a cross. It's like Jesus' cross."

"Mr. Wilkins, Dorie has made her choice. Tell us what we owe and load it for us, please."

Mr. Wilkins scratched his head and raised his eyebrows. "Okay. If you want this one, there's no charge. It was going to be scrap anyway."

A broad smile crossed Dorie's face, and she clapped her hands. "Oh, thank you. It's perfect."

The following week, the tree stood on the altar of the Chapel, ready to be decorated for Christmas. Parents and students gathered for the annual event.

Mrs. Nelson, the mother of one of the students, approached Miss Beulah and whispered, "This isn't the tree that's going to be the altar tree for Christmas, is it?"

"Yes, it's the one selected by this year's student. It's special, just as all the trees chosen by our students are."

Mrs. Nelson rolled her eyes. "It's a far cry from a proper Christmas tree. Remember last year's magnificent white pine, tall and full bodied? My Jimmy chose it. Of course, I did help him pick it out."

"Yes, I remember. Perhaps you'll appreciate the tree when you hear what the student who chose it has to say. Excuse me. I need to start the program."

Miss Beulah stepped to the lectern and addressed the audience. "As you know, it's a Chapel tradition for a middle-grade student to select the altar tree and share about his or her choice. Dorie Lambert earned the honor this year. Dorie, please come and share."

Dorie ambled to the platform with lumbering steps. She looked out over the audience and smiled at a couple seated in the first pew. She swallowed and took a breath.

"I chose this year's tree. It's different from what you might expect. I am different too. You see, I was born with a problem that made me crippled. I spent most of my life in an orphanage because no one wanted me. No one until..." Dorie stopped, drew her lips together, and cast her eyes downward. Then she looked again at the couple in the first pew. The woman smiled and wiped her eyes; the man nodded and mouthed the words, *"Go on. It's okay."*

"No one wanted me... until Charles and Mary Lambert came along and adopted me last year. They took me just as I was, and they love me just as I am." The audience applauded; even Mrs. Nelson put her hands together.

"They brought me to this church. I learned about Jesus, how He was rejected and yet loved everyone. So, when I looked for a tree to represent Christmas, I chose this one. This tree is a lot like Jesus and a little like me.

"No one wanted this tree. But I saw something special. The large limbs form a cross, reminding me of Jesus spreading out His arms in love for me and for everyone. 'For God so loved the world, that He gave His only Son, so that everyone who believes in Him will not perish, but have eternal life.' John 3:16.

"See the smaller limbs? They hang down like Jesus did on the cross. He had the burden of all our sins. See the gaps in the tree? They're just like gaps some of us have. Jesus said, 'Love one another as I have loved you.' Jesus showed His love and filled our gaps. So, maybe all this tree needs is a little love too—just like me and you."

Several people in the audience wiped their eyes as they watched Dorie hobble back to her seat. Then they stood and applauded.

Miss Beulah went to the lectern and cleared her throat. "Students, please show your love to the tree by hanging your ornaments on it. Soon it will be full of love, just like you are."

Mrs. Nelson made her way to Miss Beulah. "You were right. I'm sorry for what I said."

Miss Beulah patted her arm. "God knows. He uses what we consider to be imperfect to bless us and teach us."

"I can see that." Mrs. Nelson smiled as they watched the children hang their handmade ornaments on the tree, each one making the tree more beautiful.

"It's transforming, isn't it?" Miss Beulah's eyes were fixed on Dorie. The girl's face was radiant as she beheld her tree being transformed into the symbol of love and mercy she had always imagined it to be.

December Decorations

Man-made decorations
At every shop abound
But none are quite as lovely
As those that can be found
Outside, where there's a storehouse
For everyone to see
Holiday decorations
Made naturally—and free.
Deep blue skies of winter
Stars like candlelight
Sparkle in the heavens
With gold moon shining bright.
By day we're blessed with brilliant
Christmas reds and green
Holly berry, pine, and fir
Burst upon the scene.
A crimson cardinal and his mate
Make a striking pair
While scent of rosemary
And laurel fill the crispy air.
A winter rose may still be found
Hanging on a vine
Like a special ornament
Jack Frost left behind.

Don't fuss about adorning
Your home with purchased ware
Just look outside and marvel
At what's already there.
How could any bought décor
Compare with such as these?
The ones in God's creation
Are always sure to please!

Our Blooming Christmas Cactus

Each year we know the holidays are coming when our Christmas cactus starts to bloom. It always flowers right on time around the beginning of December, as it has faithfully for over 20 years. Blossoms sprout from the tips of its green leaves, annually refreshing our memories of the person who gave the plant to us. Her name was Marlene, and she gave us the plant when we retired and moved south at the turn of the century. She wanted to give us something that would remind us of her and her family. The cactus's blossoms do just that each year at Christmas time.

Little did we know that more than miles would soon separate us from our friend. Today, in the same room as the cactus, we have a schefflera plant that is only one or two years younger; Marlene's daughter gave it to us from her mother's funeral service in 2001. I consider both to be living legacies, reminders of a friend and friendship we treasure. While we think of her especially during the holiday season, we take solace in knowing she is spending every Christmas with Jesus, the One who came into the world and started it all.

Perhaps as you read this you are reminded of a similar memento you have from someone who is no longer with you. Maybe there is a departed loved one you also miss particularly at Christmastime. Whether it's a family member or friend, take time this holiday season to thank God for that person and for memories because memories are a gift. I feel particularly blessed that both plants are still living. I hope I can give them continued care and keep them—and the memories they represent—flourishing. I also pray I will give the same devoted care to my friends and family who are still living treasures in my life.

As the cactus blooms each year, it brings special recollections of our friend. But even as I cherish those thoughts, I'm also reminded of how wonderful Christmas is. It is an annual time to celebrate Jesus, our Savior and Lord. Unlike the cactus, He is eternal and blossoms in our lives and hearts throughout the year with His presence and love. May we all continue to remember Him daily!

How I Learned the Whole Story about Answered Prayers

I t all started last year at Christmastime when I was eleven. One Sunday, while Pastor Cornelius was preaching, he said: "God's greatest gift was the gift of His Son, and it was an answer to many prayers. It still is. God met our greatest need on that first Christmas, and He will meet your needs now if you ask—not just at Christmas but throughout the whole year." Then he asked us to bow our heads for the offering prayer, asking God to bless the church through the tithes and offerings of the congregation.

Mama sighed and took a few small bills from her purse. I knew she wished she could give more. I tried to keep my head down during the prayer, but I couldn't help peeking to see if Mr. Phillips put anything in the offering plate. He was the owner of the general store where Mama worked. I thought he was the richest man in town. I reckoned he had lots to share, but each week I noticed he simply passed the plate along when it came to him.

As we filed out after the service, Mama shook the pastor's hand and thanked him for reminding us about sharing our gifts.

I asked Mama as we left the church, "Do you think people here can answer the pastor's prayer by sharing?" The small farming town where we lived had been hit hard by the drought that had swept through Kansas over the summer, taking almost everything with it. It had been a bleak harvest season. People could barely keep food on the table, much less have anything extra to give to anyone else.

"God always provides, son, when we pray and we show our gratitude by sharing," Mama said, as she often did. She said that even after Papa died. "God answered my prayer for a job and gave you strength to help so we could keep our farm. Papa always prayed for a good harvest so he could give a portion to God, and God answered his prayers many times with enough to share with others too. God wants to bless us, and He meets our needs when we ask in faith."

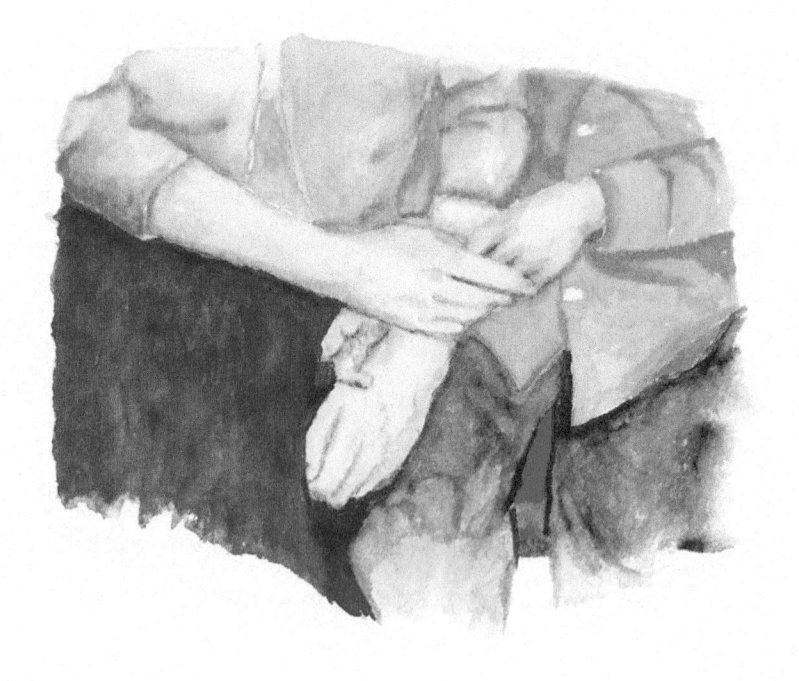

Christmas came and went, and Mama continued to pray about everything. She kept a list, and every morning I would find her hunched over her Bible murmuring prayers before she went to work.

After the New Year, something mysterious happened. People began receiving gifts out of the blue. Most were customers who Mama chatted with at the general store. Folks would share a need with her, and Mama would pray with them right there, asking God to provide. Within a week or so, packages containing just what those people needed would arrive from an anonymous sender. Attached would be an unsigned card that said, "Christmas blessings to you!" This continued to happen even though it was well past Christmas.

Mama loved telling me the stories. "Nora Piper said her husband broke the ax handle he needed to chop wood. So, guess what came in the post today for Mr. Piper?"

"A hoe?" I grinned.

"Funny boy. And remember how Mrs. Winters needed a special brace for her bad leg, but they couldn't afford it right away?"

"Let me guess. The brace showed up at the store. Are you going to tell me God sent it?"

"Yes, I believe He did. We just don't know how. Mr. Phillips says God is good and answers prayers."

"Mr. Phillips could help if he wanted to, but I think he's a scrooge."

"Why would you say such a thing?"

"He doesn't ever put anything in the Sunday offering. I see him just pass the plate."

Mama took my face in her hands and glued her eyes to mine. "Son, do you remember when Papa was sick, and we didn't know it? Remember how the doctor said afterwards Papa wouldn't go and get the medicine he needed because we needed the money for seed? We didn't know how sick Papa was until it was too late because he kept it hidden. Sometimes, son, we don't know the whole story."

Mama wiped her eyes and mine with her apron. "God is good and answers prayers."

The answered prayers kept coming, and Mama shared the stories every time. Homer Parker received a new harness for his plow horse after one broke. Millie Haller received three chickens to replace the ones a fox had taken. Hannah Morris gave birth to twins instead of just one baby and needed extra clothes and formula; she received a big box full of just what Mama prayed for. On and on the provisions came long throughout the New Year. Even as the weather started to warm, the anonymous notes on the gifts continued to say "Christmas blessings to you!"

The drought ended that spring when welcoming rain came to the thirsty land. Farmers planted new seed, and the crops came in good measure. People thanked God for sending a good harvest and shared its blessings with one another.

It was a wonderful year, and we expected to have an equally wonderful Christmas. But then, just before the holiday, the accident happened. Mr. Phillips was unloading a wagon when one of the horses spooked. The wagon tipped over and fell on him, killing him instantly. It was an awful tragedy. I think Mama cried as much then as she did when Papa died.

Mr. Phillips' son, Wyeth, came, and Pastor Cornelius asked him to speak at the funeral. He told the congregation about how much his father loved and cared for him and his family and how generous he was.

"My father was blessed. He made a small fortune in Topeka and wanted to share it. He bought the general store here, came to know you people, and decided to stay. He said he could see God working in the hearts of people. Last year, he told me about Pastor Cornelius's sermon, how we should celebrate Christmas throughout the year and pray for our needs and the needs of others to be fulfilled. So, when he heard of a need, he would contact me and I'd send what was needed. But the funny thing was, he didn't want the credit. He said, 'God blessed me, so He should get the credit.' He never told anyone and always had me sign the card with 'Christmas blessings to you.' He even gave his tithe to the church in secret."

I gasped and looked at Mama. She smiled and squeezed my hand.

Wyeth wiped his eyes and added, "He didn't want any praise or thanks to go to him. That's the kind of man he was. I share this with you today to honor him and to honor God, whom my father loved and served."

That's how I learned the whole story about prayers and how God sometimes uses people to answer them. Like Mama says, God is good and answers prayers. We may not know how He does it, but He does it for our good and His glory.

Every Day is Christmas

ackson Turner had a way with flowers. Some said he could coax a rose blossom out of a dead thorn bush and turn brown grass into green just by walking on it. Jackson was the new owner of Four Seasons Flower Shop, and word of his horticultural expertise soon spread throughout the small town of Harpersville. The most unusual thing about Jackson, however, was the way he greeted people. No matter what day of the year or time of day, he always greeted everyone with a hearty "Merry Christmas!"

Some people looked at him as if they hadn't heard him correctly; others shook their heads in disdain. Some responded with chuckles, while others gave replies like "Bah! Humbug!" or "You crazy, man? It's July!" or "Happy New Year to you too!"

No one seemed interested enough to ask him why he gave such a greeting; no one, that is, until ten-year-old Polly Parks came to his shop.

When the bell on the shop door announced Polly's entrance, Jackson turned to greet her. "Merry Christmas, young lady!" he beamed.

Polly just stared. She had heard about his weird way of saying "hello."

"May I help you with something?"

"I'd like to buy a rose for my mother."

"Ah, and what is the special occasion?"

"It's not an occasion. She's sick."

"Oh, I'm sorry to hear that." Jackson's voice dropped. "But you came to the right place. I have the most beautiful rose grown especially for your mother."

"Is it red?"

"Indeed! Red is the right color to make anyone feel better."

"Can I ask you something?" Polly folded her arms.

"Most certainly."

"Why do you say 'Merry Christmas' when it's not Christmas?"

"What is your name, young lady?"

"Polly Parks."

"Well, Miss Polly Parks, if you will sit on the stool here while I prepare the rose for your mother, I'll tell you why I say 'Merry Christmas.'"

Polly climbed up on the stool and watched Jackson begin trimming the long-stemmed rose.

"On that first Christmas Day long ago, God sent a baby into the world to an ordinary couple. But the baby was not ordinary. He was God's son."

"I know. It was Jesus," Polly chimed in.

"Oh, then perhaps you know the story."

"I know all about it. God sent Him to save the people of the world from their sin."

"That's right. Do you know how He did that, Polly?"

"He died on the cross, right? And then He came back to life."

"Do you believe Jesus died for you?"

"Yes, I took Jesus into my heart last year and asked Him to forgive my sins. I've been baptized too."

"Well, Miss Polly, then you should know that because Jesus came that first Christmas, every day is Christmas for those who have received Him as their Savior."

"So, that's why you say it?"

"Exactly. When I say 'Merry Christmas,' I want to remind everyone who Jesus is and why He came. Some people make fun of me, and rarely someone will ask me about it like you did. But there's a song I wrote that says it well. I'm not the best singer, but here goes."

Jackson lifted his voice and sang:

Every day is Christmas,
It's not just once a year
For those who follow Jesus
He's with us now, right here.

Christmas is His birthday
But that is just a start
'Cause every day is Christmas
When you have Him in your heart.

So, I say "Merry Christmas"
As I greet each one today
Yes, I say "Merry Christmas"
'Cause it's Christmas every day!

Polly clapped her hands in appreciation. "I like it! And your singing is fine."

"Thank you." Jackson bowed. "So, Miss Polly, like the song says, every day truly is Christmas for those who give their hearts to Jesus."

He handed Polly the red rose wrapped in green paper and tied with red ribbon.

"How much do I owe you?"

"Nothing. It's my pleasure to share the meaning of my greeting and to share this rose with you and your mother," he smiled. "You could say it's a Christmas gift."

Polly giggled. "Then I'll just say thank you. And by the way, Merry Christmas to you!" Polly skipped out the door and hurried home.

"Polly, is that you?" her mother called from the bedroom when she heard the front door open.

"Merry Christmas, Momma!" Polly burst into the room.

"Merry Christmas? Why on earth would you say that in July?"

"I'm glad you asked." She handed the rose to her mother. "As soon as I get a vase, I'll share the whole story."

Jackson Turner had a way with flowers and with people. Soon, many people in Harpersville began to greet each other in a most unconventional fashion, saying "Merry Christmas," no matter the time of year. It was a way of reminding themselves and each other that every day is the Lord's. Every day is Christmas.

Afterword

T he stories and illustrations in this book come from our hearts to yours, dear reader. But none of them could have been written or drawn without the greatest—and truest—Christmas story taking place. That story is found in another book, the Bible:

In prophecy – "Therefore the Lord himself will give you a sign. Behold, the virgin shall conceive and bear a son, and shall call his name Immanuel." (Isaiah 7:14 ESV)

"But you, Bethlehem Ephrathah, though you are small among the clans of Judah, out of you will come for me one who will be ruler over Israel, whose origins are from of old, from ancient times." (Micah 5:2 ESV)

In proclamation – "And in the same region there were shepherds out in the field, keeping watch over their flock by night. And an angel of the Lord appeared to them, and the glory of the Lord shone around them, and they were filled with fear. And the angel said to them, 'Fear not, for behold, I bring you good news of great joy that will be for all the people. For unto you is born this day in the city of David a Savior, who is Christ the Lord. And this will be a sign for you: you will find a baby wrapped in swaddling cloths and lying in a manger.' And suddenly there was with the angel a multitude of the heavenly host praising God and saying, 'Glory to God in the highest, and on earth peace among those with whom he is pleased!'" (Luke 2:8-14 ESV)

In purpose – "For God so loved the world, that he gave his only Son, that whoever believes in him should not perish but have eternal life. For God did not send his Son into the world to condemn the world, but in order that the world might be saved through him. Whoever believes in him is not condemned, but whoever does not believe is condemned already, because he has not believed in the name of the only Son of God." (John 3:16-18 ESV)

"But when Christ had offered for all time a single sacrifice for sins, he sat down at the right hand of God." (Hebrews 10:12 ESV)

In promise — "Jesus said to her, 'I am the resurrection and the life. Whoever believes in me, though he die, yet shall he live, and everyone who lives and believes in me shall never die. Do you believe this?'" (John 11:25-26 ESV)

"Let not your hearts be troubled. Believe in God; believe also in me. In my Father's house are many rooms. If it were not so, would I have told you that I go to prepare a place for you? And if I go and prepare a place for you, I will come again and will take you to myself, that where I am you may be also." (John 14:1-3 ESV)

Christmas! What started long ago when the Son of God came to earth will forever be celebrated. It's a daily blessing for those who not only know about Christmas but also have a relationship with the Christ of Christmas. If you are someone who only knows the Christmas story and would like to know how to have a personal relationship with God, please visit this website: www.peacewithGod.net

Merry Christmas today and always, everyone! And remember that every day is Christmas!

Acknowledgements

No author writes and publishes a book without the help of many supporters, and I am no exception. I have friends who encourage me to write; my husband, Craig, who gives me time and space to do so; and my Sandhills Writers group who reviews my stories and helps me refine them. I'm grateful to all these special people.

There are also specific individuals who have made this project a blessing. Rachel Greene, who formatted my first two books, *Seasons in the Garden* and *My Faithbook Messages*, has taken on both the editing and formatting of *Every Day is Christmas*. Rachel has done a wonderful job of fine-tuning my stories and presenting a layout that pleases the reader. I'm also indebted to Joan Silvestri, who proofread the manuscript more than once throughout my writing process to be sure it was in its best form.

Although I've said it many times, it bears repeating again: Becky Guinn's artistic rendering of each story brings them to life. I am forever grateful to her for all the time and care she put into her beautiful illustrations. In addition, Becky's daughter, Amy Guinn, a talented graphic designer, used her photographic expertise to make sure each painting was captured in a digital form best suitable for the book. Find out more about Amy's work at www.theartisticmoment.com and www.shookguinn.com.

It should be obvious that I could not produce anything of merit without the presence of the LORD Jesus in my life. He is the inspiration for every story of value that gives glory to God.

Finally, I am most grateful to you, the reader, for turning these pages and reading the book!

Meet the Author

Sandra Fischer – Christ-lover, former teacher and
Christian bookstore owner, wife, mother, grandmother.

Sandra is a native of Indiana who became a southern transplant on Dataw Island, SC, in 2001 when she and her husband retired. Her first book, *Seasons in the Garden*, is a collection of inspirational poetry and prose written over fourteen years for the Dataw Garden Club monthly newsletter. In 2016, she relocated to Southern Pines, NC, and joined the NC Writers Network and Sandhills Writers Group. Her second book, *My Faithbook Messages: Devotions to Like and Share*, is a collection of devotionals written for FaithWriters.com, where she is a premium member. *Every Day is Christmas* is her latest work. All her books are available through Amazon and Barnes & Noble or can be ordered directly from the author. Additional short stories and articles by Sandra appear in various anthologies, which can be found on her Amazon author page.

To read more about Sandra and her writing, visit:
www.amzn.com/Sandra-Fischer/e/B00ISC2GA4
www.facebook.com/sandrafischerinspires
FaithWriters.com Member Profile
www.sandifischer.com

Meet the Illustrator

Becky Guinn – Christ-lover, artist, teacher, illustrator, speaker, wife, mother, grandmother, friend.

Becky has loved art from the time she was three years old. Her mother encouraged her, and a 4th grade teacher guided her on the path to become a professional artist. She earned a degree in art education and was pursuing a master's degree when she was named "Teacher of the Year" at Valley High School in Alabama in 2002.

The next day, she entered the hospital for a heart procedure that would impact her life. After suffering an allergic reaction to medication, all four of Becky's limbs were amputated to save her life. Through rehab, many prayers, and the support of family and friends, Becky returned to teach at Valley High and completed her master's degree.

With special equipment, Becky continues to paint beautiful artwork, driven by determination to create with her mechanical hands. After leaving her school position, she started a statewide program called "Hooked on Art" to teach and inspire children. She now tours the country, going wherever God calls her to share her testimony and talent.

To find out more about Becky's art and life story, visit:

www.beckyguinn.org

Made in the USA
Columbia, SC
23 October 2021